Beauty
and the
Beast

CANDLEWICK PRESS
CAMBRIDGE, MASSACHUSETTS

Beauty
and the
Beast

retold by
MAX EILENBERG

illustrated by
ANGELA BARRETT

Once upon a time, there was an extremely wealthy merchant who lived in an extremely splendid house with his three extremely beloved daughters. Ernest Fortune was his name — or rather, Ernest Jeremiah Augustus Fortune, Esquire, Merchant, as it said on his business card.

Mr. Fortune was a very successful businessman, and he had two favorite sayings. "Fortune by name, fortune by nature" was one, always said with a broad smile and a merry crinkling of his eyes as he rattled the coins in his pocket. "I simply can't say no to my girls" was the other — at which he'd hold up his hands and dip his head with a pleased look that suggested he was anything but sorry about it, for the three girls were the very apples of Mr. Fortune's eye. He couldn't have loved them more, he would tell you, each in her own special way, as he pulled from his pocket the precious pictures he always carried with him, ready to show anyone who was interested and even some who weren't.

"This one's Gertrude," he would say, "my eldest. Charming girl, loads of fun, loves her jewels, hopeless with money, spoil her rotten." And if you looked a little more closely at Gertrude's picture, Mr. Fortune might point out the gorgeous diamond necklace she wore, and the splendid emerald earrings. "Cost me a pretty penny, I can tell you," he'd say proudly, "but" (and you'd know it was coming) "I simply can't say no to my girls."

Now you might consider that Gertrude in fact looked a little spoiled and not very grateful—but already Mr. Fortune would have handed over the next picture. "Hermione," he'd say. "Absolutely lovely, smashing girl, mad about clothes, height of fashion, dreadfully expensive, never refuse her." And if you looked a little more closely at Hermione's picture, Mr. Fortune might point out the glimmering silken dress she wore, and the very impressive hat. "Cost me an arm and a leg," he'd say, smiling happily, "but—well, what can you do?"

And here you might reflect that Hermione looked, in fact, rather mean and somewhat overdressed—but Mr. Fortune would have moved on again. "Beauty," he would begin—but here, quite unexpectedly, his voice would break, his eyes would start to water, and a tear would roll down his plump,

rosy cheek. Then he would pause for a moment, as if to collect himself. "Always reminds me of her poor, dear mother," he would say quietly, at which Mr. Fortune would smile bravely and blow his nose  loudly while you looked a little more closely at Beauty's picture.

She was a girl of such simple, radiant beauty that it would take your breath away. There were no expensive jewels or fine fabrics for Mr. Fortune to point out—she needed none. Her skin itself was smooth as pearls and her hair as fine as silk, and her large, smiling eyes shone straight at yours, full of life and a warmth as generous as the sun's.

"A treasure," Mr. Fortune would tell you, "kind as can be, spoils me rotten, never asks for a thing. Love to buy her presents; won't let me. Doesn't matter—always looks fabulous. Beauty by name, beauty by nature, I suppose; couldn't wish for more."

And that, you might think, was worth more than all the money in the world, for with three such beloved daughters Mr. Fortune could surely look forward to a long, happy, comfortable, and untroubled life.

But there you would be wrong, for appearances can be deceptive, and that is where our story really begins. . . .

*I*t all started one summer, on a perfect—and perfectly normal—day. The birds sang and the sun shone on the magnificent town square where the Fortunes lived in their enormous house. Mr. Fortune left for work early, as usual, picked up by his coachman in his luxurious carriage, and the three girls passed the morning as they always did.

Hermione and Gertrude adorned themselves with their finest finery and entertained the many young bachelors who courted them each day with invitations to balls and dinners and glamorous parties. Indeed, they had so many invitations that they sometimes went to three or four parties in one evening—which perhaps explained why they were both growing a little plumper than they used to be, though their outfits were so dazzling you would hardly notice. Certainly the young men seemed not to, nor did they appear to mind that Hermione and Gertrude were often very rude to them and always, without so much as a "thank you," greedily gulped the chocolates the bachelors

brought as presents, without offering any to anybody else at all, ever.

But Hermione and Gertrude were so wealthy and the young men so eager to marry them that no amount of rudeness could put them off.

While her sisters were entertaining, Beauty would run up and down the stairs every time the bell rang, answering the door and greeting all the visitors. Hermione and Gertrude never thanked her for it. Still, Beauty was glad to see them so popular, though she wished that the young men weren't quite so obviously interested in their riches. Beauty was too young to have any admirers herself, but in any case, her own heart was set on marrying not for money, but for love. She dreamed of the day when she would be swept off her feet by some irresistibly fine and handsome young suitor: a prince among men, and quite probably a real prince as well. For Beauty had no doubt that such a day would come; she'd read enough love stories, all of which involved marrying a prince and living happily ever after. And you never knew when that prince might come to your door.

Now of course real life doesn't always work out like that, but Beauty was still young and romantic and full of dreams. So you can imagine her shock when once more the bell rang and once more she ran to answer it, full of her secret hopes of love—and there before her stood her father.

At least, she *thought* it was her father—but it took a moment to recognize him. In the few hours he'd been away, Mr. Fortune had altered completely, as if he had suddenly aged many years; he had shrunk into himself, a ghost of the father she knew. He looked pale and worn, and so ill with worry that Beauty feared he would fall down on the steps before her very eyes.

"Papa!" she gasped, taking him by the arm and leading him to the nearest chair, where he sat, slumped, while Beauty called to her sisters to come quickly and the young men hurried from the house, making their excuses and averting their eyes as if some awful shame or sickness might infect them if they lingered.

"Oh, my dear children," groaned Mr. Fortune when at last they were all gathered around him. "I have a terrible tale to tell you."

And so the story came out, as evening fell and the family sat huddled in a deepening gloom. It had been a dreadful, disastrous day at Mr. Fortune's office. Fires had burned his warehouses; storms had sunk his ships.

Within hours everything was lost: his business collapsed, his savings were gone, and still he owed more than he could pay. In a word, he was ruined, and the name of Fortune was just a cruel mockery. To pay the debts, they must sell the house, all the fine paintings and furniture, the clothes and jewels—everything, in short, would have to go, and they would flee the town the very next day to find cheap lodging in the country wherever they could.

"But what will become of us?" cried Hermione and Gertrude. "Oh, Father, how could you?"

Mr. Fortune shook his head in silent misery, and Beauty wrapped her arms around him. "Don't worry, Papa," she said. "We'll be all right."

"Don't be so ridiculous, you stupid little girl," Hermione snapped furiously. *"Nothing's ever going to be all right again."*

There were no admiring young men to wave them off next morning as the unhappy Fortunes set out in a sad, single cart pulled by their oldest, lamest horse. There was no sun to warm them, no birdsong to lift their spirits; it was a bleak, gray day with a bitter wind that blew, as if overnight the summer had turned to cruel winter. And there was no bright glitter of diamonds or rustle of fine silk—only one thin blanket to shelter them, and the constant wailing of Hermione and Gertrude.

Three cold days and colder nights they traveled, far from the city and

deep into the country. It was a terrible journey through stony fields, on roads churned to mud in the endless, stinging rain. Strange, suspicious faces glared at them from behind closed windows; angry dogs chased them on their way. At last, exhausted, hungry, and chilled to the bone, they found a place to stop. It was a small, run-down cottage with a tiny garden overgrown with weeds and thorns—but it did not matter, for they were so tired they could not move another step, and the cottage seemed to welcome them as if it were their home.

And home it became over the weeks and months that followed as the Fortunes tried to make the best of their new life. Hermione and Gertrude grumbled all the time, for they hated being poor and refused to get their hands dirty, but Beauty worked hard to help her father, and soon the cottage was clean and warm and the garden cleared and planted. There was a stable for the horse and enough food for them all. But each evening as they sat around the fire, a gloomy silence settled over the Fortune family, for the sad truth was that not a single one of them was happy.

Hermione and Gertrude, of course, loathed it all. How could their father have been so selfish and stupid as to lose all his money? What would become of them now? Why shouldn't they have lovely clothes and jewels? Didn't he understand how many parties they were missing?

Mr. Fortune was miserable too. How he longed to cheer his daughters with glorious surprises, but he didn't have a penny to his name. Once he couldn't say no to his girls; now he couldn't say yes. Hermione and Gertrude seemed to be growing more short-tempered by the day; even Beauty, the lovely, kind Beauty, though she worked hard and tried to be cheerful, sometimes could not hide her sadness, and that made Mr. Fortune feel worse than anything.

For Beauty *was* sad. She was sorry for her father, of course, and for her sisters, but it was more than that. The cottage was fine and the country was pretty and she didn't mind the work, but, oh, it was so lonely and so quiet. Nothing ever happened. There were no visitors now, no bells ringing, no doors to open with a secret hope of being swept off her feet, head over heels in love. It was becoming clear to Beauty, as the months went by, that no handsome young prince was ever going to knock on the door of their little cottage.

So it was a rather unhappy Beauty who came downstairs one morning a whole year later to find that a message had arrived from the city with wonderful, unexpected news: a ship had docked that had been thought lost at sea, and some of the cargo might be Mr. Fortune's. They would be rich again! Mr. Fortune prepared to leave at once and kissed the girls good-bye, promising to bring each a splendid present.

"S-s-silks," simpered Hermione, almost overcome with excitement.

"P-p-pearls," whimpered Gertrude, barely able to speak for joy.

"And Beauty?" said Mr. Fortune, turning to his youngest daughter.

But Beauty's dreams could not be bought. "Nothing, thank you," she murmured, "but your safe return."

"That you shall have," he answered. "But *nothing*?" There was sorrow in his voice, for he knew how unhappy his daughter had become. "Come now—I would bring you anything."

I would like a prince, thought Beauty, and then she looked up, ashamed to have disappointed him. Her father loved giving presents. Desperately she tried to think of something—anything. "I am sorry, Father. If it would please you, I would like a rose. They do not grow here, and I miss them very much."

Her sisters could hardly contain their disgust. "What a waste!" they whispered furiously to each other. "Stupid goody-goody. What's she playing at?" But they dared not say anything in front of their father, and he was thrilled.

"You shall have the finest rose money can buy!" exclaimed Mr. Fortune, and with that, he was on his way, as fast as his horse could carry him.

When Mr. Fortune reached the city, however, things did not turn out as he had hoped. He still owed money. The cargo from the ship was seized to pay his debts, and in spite of a great deal of trouble and effort, he left for home a few days later empty-handed and just as poor as he had come.

It was a tiring journey, and he was some thirty miles from the cottage, looking forward to seeing his daughters again and worrying only about how he would tell them the bad news, when, as night fell, the wind grew cold and a terrible blizzard blew up. Mr. Fortune sought shelter in a great forest, but the weather was so dreadful and the trees were so dense that he was soon completely lost. Exhausted now, he clung to the horse's neck as best he could while icy branches knocked him

hard at every step, and in the awful howling of the wind he seemed to hear the cries of wolves circling greedily, just waiting for the moment, not far off, when he would surely fall and die.

All seemed hopeless, when at last he saw a distant gleam of light dimly shining through the wood. Stumbling, Mr. Fortune followed it, as the trees thinned and the light grew stronger, until suddenly he was out of the forest. Then, in one unforgettable instant, the bitter wind dropped all at once and the still, crisp air was filled with the warm scent of a thousand orange trees, which were glowing in the astonishing brightness of a gigantic palace lit at every window from top to bottom.

Mr. Fortune gazed in wonder as his horse carried him across the smooth, thick, white carpet of snow, all sounds muffled.

Beyond the great carpet of snow, Mr. Fortune rode down an avenue of trees hung with bells and lanterns, past sweeping lawns and flower beds and hedges shaped like fabulous creatures that might almost have been alive, while at every step songbirds sang as if to greet him.

The palace itself was too large, too dazzling to take in all at once. It seemed to go on forever, with countless wings and windows, towers and turrets, all in perfect proportion and on a scale far greater and more beautiful than anything Mr. Fortune had ever seen. And it had a splendid stable; his horse had walked right into it and found it full of hay and oats and warm, dry bedding. Mr. Fortune left him munching happily and made his way to the huge front door of the palace.

There he stood for a moment, expecting that in such a place there would be footmen or servants to welcome him, but none came. Surprised, Mr. Fortune raised his hand instead to the door knocker, studded with precious stones and carved from solid gold. It was larger than a man's head and looked impossibly heavy, but as he touched it, the great door swung silently open, and Mr. Fortune entered the palace.

He found himself in a vast entrance hall, enchantingly furnished and lit by thousands of sparkling candles, their reflections shimmering on every surface. A warm fire blazed in an enormous hearth, and Mr. Fortune hurried forward to dry himself, for his clothes were still cold and wet. At the far end of the room he noticed a table set for one person, with a meal that looked and smelled almost unbearably delicious. *Perhaps whoever lives here will offer me some,* he thought, but after an hour, when the clock struck ten and no one had appeared, the famished Mr. Fortune could stand it no longer. He sat down and feasted on the finest supper he had ever tasted, accompanied by several glasses of the most excellent wine. Afterward he was very tired, and so, feeling now really quite at home, he made his way up the immense staircase in search of a bed. Finding at once a door that opened onto a sumptuous four-poster, he lay down and fell straight to sleep.

It was late the next morning before Mr. Fortune awoke, fully refreshed from his deep slumber. When he turned to dress, imagine his astonishment on finding that his old clothes had been replaced by a brand-new suit that fitted so well it might have been tailor-made for him. "Well," he mused aloud, "this is very fine. Fortune by nature, indeed." And then he smiled. "Or perhaps some kind fairy lives here who has taken a shine to me!"

Rather pleased with this amusing thought, Mr. Fortune went downstairs to the great hall, and having thoroughly enjoyed the lavish breakfast that seemed to be laid out for him, he spoke to the empty room: "Thank you, kind fairy, for your very generous hospitality. You have a splendid house. I must be on my way now, but please do call on our humble abode whenever you're passing." And, feeling very cheerful, Mr. Fortune went out to find his horse.

The way to the stable seemed a little different from the night before, and Mr. Fortune found himself in a part of the garden he had not previously noticed. It was given over entirely to roses: red roses of the most exquisite loveliness and perfection, their color brilliant against the whiteness of the ground, their red petals streaked with snow, and with a fragrance so strong and heady it seemed to lull the very songbirds. As he enjoyed their scent, Mr. Fortune remembered Beauty's request. Delighted to be able to bring at least one of his daughters the gift she had asked for, he selected the finest, reddest, most beautiful rose he could see and, with the very greatest care and attention, snapped it smartly off.

Oh, Mr. Fortune,
you unhappy man.

All at once, the sky darkened as if a shadow had fallen across the world. The earth shook, the songbirds flew off, screeching, and a howl of pain and anger filled the air. Mr. Fortune started to turn, but a huge, clawed fist seized his shoulder and spun him around like a rag doll, to face a creature so ugly that Mr. Fortune almost fainted with fright.

"How dare you? How dare you steal my rose?" it growled. "I saved your life"—it spat out the words like a sour taste—"and in return you stole my rose." The terrible eyes blazed with rage. "You will pay for it with your life: prepare to die!"

"I beg you," pleaded Mr. Fortune in horror, barely able to control his voice, "forgive me, please. It was an innocent mistake. My daughter wanted a rose; it is for her. I meant no harm. You have been so kind, my lord—"

"Do not call me 'lord'!" roared the creature. "Do not try to flatter me with pretty words. I do not like it. We should say what we mean and be what we are. I am a beast. My name is Beast. You will call me Beast. Beast by nature, Beast by name. Beast! Beast! Beast!" He shuddered as if trying to control himself, and then he pointed at the cowering Mr. Fortune. "You say you have a daughter?"

"Yes, my—Beast," stammered the desperate man. "Three—I can show you their pictures—"

"Don't!" spat the Beast. "Pictures mean nothing. I want your life; but I will take your daughter instead. Then you may live—but she must come of her own free will. I give you one day.

Go now and bring her, or return alone and die. Swear to do this, or I will kill you at once!"

"I swear on my life," answered Mr. Fortune hastily, thinking this way at least he would have the chance to say farewell to his beloved girls before returning to meet his fate.

"Then go," said the Beast, turning away. "There are some gifts with your horse. I would not leave your daughters empty-handed."

As the Beast lumbered slowly off, Mr. Fortune ran as fast as he could for the stables, desperate to get away. His horse was waiting for him, with a brand-new saddle and harness, and on its back was strapped a great trunk, full of more fine dresses and jewelry than his daughters could ever have imagined. But no riches could comfort Mr. Fortune as the horse carried him home, for the Beast had broken his heart.

It was Beauty who saw him first, a small, dark smudge in the broad, white landscape. "He's coming!" she called. "He's here!" At once Hermione and Gertrude ran out ahead of her, desperate for their presents, screaming with delight at the sight of Mr. Fortune's handsome new suit, too excited to notice the tears running down his cheeks. They threw open the lid of the magnificent trunk and—oh, what joy! What precious things! What ecstasy of wealth was theirs!

But as Mr. Fortune gave Beauty her rose, his voice was cracked with grief. "My darling Beauty," he said, "your present has cost me more than any treasure." And then out poured the whole story of his ordeal.

They listened in horror, scarcely able to believe that such a monster could exist. Perhaps poverty and their father's disappointment in the city had simply driven him mad, but gradually Mr. Fortune convinced them that he was speaking the absolute truth. Then horror gave way to

anger, and anger quickly turned to blame. Beauty's sisters glared at her.

"You always have to be different, don't you," Hermione said bitterly. "Why couldn't you ask for something normal?"

"'Bring me a rose, Papa, bring me a rose,'" mocked Gertrude. "You think you're so special, and now you've ruined everything."

But Beauty didn't say anything. She hardly even heard their words. *It is no one's fault but mine,* she was thinking. Her beloved father was in terrible trouble, all because of her. *He will not die,* she thought. *The rose is mine. I will go. I will gladly go.* And then, as if she were waking from a deep sleep, she suddenly spoke out. "Father," she said, "don't be sad. You picked the rose for me, and I will go to this Beast."

They all looked at her in astonishment. "No, Beauty," said her father.

"Yes, Father," she said with a firmness that surprised everyone, even herself. "I know what I must do, and my mind is made up."

And however much they argued, late into the night, there was no changing Beauty's mind; even if her father tried to set off alone, she said, she would follow him. By the time they fell asleep, too tired to talk any more, it was settled. Beauty would meet the Beast.

It was early the next morning and still dark when Beauty and her father left home. They rode all day, huddled together for warmth, through snow-packed fields and icy forest, until night fell and the magnificent palace appeared before them. In the stables there was fresh hay again; then Mr. Fortune led Beauty to the vast hall where the candles shone like fireflies and the logs blazed in the hearth and the great table, this time, was set for two.

They picked at the food in unhappy, nervous silence. Mr. Fortune was too sad to speak, and Beauty, though she wanted to be brave, felt horribly frightened, knowing that soon the Beast would come. She did not have long to wait. She felt it first, like a cold darkness in the room: something was watching.

And then she gasped as the monstrous creature emerged, towering high above them, its claws dragging across the floor with a screech that set her teeth on edge and its sour smell catching at her nose. It was unspeakably ugly, and it spoke, or rather growled, in a voice so hoarse it hurt her to listen.

"Did you choose to come here of your own free will?" the Beast asked.

Beauty could hardly speak for trembling, but she managed to nod her head.

"Then you are welcome," said the Beast. It breathed in deeply, as if it would say more to her, but instead it turned abruptly to Mr. Fortune. "Your daughter's love has saved your life. Say good-bye before you sleep. You will leave before she wakes."

There was silence. The sound had gone; the smell had gone; the Beast had gone. Beauty stared after him. *How strange,* she thought. *He could not look at me.* It made no sense, but at least she was alive and hadn't fainted with fear. "It will be all right," she whispered to her weeping father. "It will be all right." And they fell asleep where they sat, worn out with tension and grief.

When Beauty raised her head from the table the next morning, she knew that she was on her own. She sat absolutely still for a moment, her heart quaking as she thought of the monster who held her prisoner. "He will not break my spirit," she vowed. "I will not show him any fear—only that I despise him for his cruelty and loathe him for his ugliness."

And having made this brave decision, Beauty stood and made her way upstairs to find a room in which she might unpack her small case from home. She felt dwarfed by the enormous staircase and, at the top, by the echoing vastness of the great passageway that led off it in each direction as far as the eye could see. As she hesitated, unsure which way to turn, she saw a door straight in front of her on which, as if in a glowing magic hand, were written the words *Beauty's Room*.

So this is my prison cell, thought Beauty gloomily, turning the handle and stepping into a room that was so unlike anything she had imagined that she thought she must be dreaming. It was not a cell at all:

not dark or dank or tiny or cold. There were no heavy manacles hanging from the walls or iron bars across filthy windows. It was instead quite the most astonishingly luxurious room Beauty had ever seen—or rather, series of rooms, for each led into another, all as splendid as the last. The gorgeous bedroom with its vast, plump bed led to the dressing room, where tall wardrobes were filled with marvelous outfits, all a perfect fit. There was a huge, warm bathroom with scented oils of every color, and a bright sitting room, with enough soft sofas and rugs for every day of the year. In the music room waited an entire orchestra of harpsichords and violins and cellos and flutes and oboes, all humming quietly in tune as Beauty entered, as if to say, "Welcome—let's play," and a great dance floor stretched invitingly across the room. A great library was stacked floor to ceiling with every book she had ever heard of and many more she hadn't. Beauty gazed around in delight and gasped, and put her hand to her mouth and said, "Oh!"

For suddenly it occurred to her that the Beast would never have gone to so much trouble if he meant to kill her—at least, not immediately—and

so she might as well enjoy it while it lasted.

My only wish, she thought, *is that I could see my beloved father and my dear sisters,* and immediately there appeared a mirror on the wall in which, to her astonishment, she saw Mr. Fortune safely back home, while Hermione and Gertrude paraded before him in their new finery. "Thank you, Beast," said Beauty to herself. "You are kinder than you look."

By the time Beauty had finished exploring and delighting in every marvelous detail, it was growing dark. At once candles flickered into light, and by their warm glow she treated herself to a luxuriously foamy bath; then she selected a perfectly exquisite dress from the wardrobe and went downstairs to supper.

The great hall looked magnificent in the candlelight, and a delicious meal was laid out on the table. But as Beauty took her seat, the clock chimed nine and there came the terrible, dragging sound of the Beast's approach, and she felt sick with a fear that she struggled not to show as he appeared.

For a moment there was silence while Beauty prayed he would not harm her, but then the Beast spoke in his slow, rasping voice: "Beauty," he said, "may I join you?"

Beauty's head spun, and for a moment she thought she would faint. What did he want? What was she meant to say? Then she summoned all her courage, looked straight at him—heavens, he was ugly—and answered as calmly as she could. "I'm sure you'll do whatever you want," she said, surprising herself with her boldness and immediately worrying that she might have made him angry.

"No," he answered shortly, as if trying to control himself. "Everything here is for your pleasure alone. I will leave you if you wish."

Beauty was amazed. Could he mean it? But before she could answer, he went on, his face twisted away from hers: "I hope you like your rooms. I can tell you find me too ugly to bear in any case."

"Yes—no," stammered Beauty, not wanting to lie or offend, for he seemed almost to be in pain. "That is, you seem very kind and your palace is lovely—but it is true that you are—"

"I am hideous," said the Beast angrily, rising to his feet as if he could not bear to be with her any longer.

"Perhaps," said Beauty. She was shocked by the bitterness in his voice and groped for some words of comfort. "But looks aren't everything, and—"

"Aren't they?" he snapped, and suddenly the atmosphere was very different: threatening, uncertain, dangerous. Beauty shrank back, the hairs rising on her neck as the Beast leaned toward her.

She could see him with awful clarity now; he was so close: the great, strong teeth, the huge nose, the pitiless eyes in which she saw herself reflected like a tiny flower floating on a deep, black pond. As she gazed in fear, she heard the Beast speak: "Then will you marry me?"

Beauty stared in horror, barely able to make sense of the words. "No," she shrieked, "no, leave me alone; no!"

In the Beast's eyes, she saw her reflection shimmer as the black pond brimmed with tears, and then the Beast turned away with a sigh that echoed around the great hall and up the stairs until it filled the whole palace with sorrow. "Farewell, Beauty," said the Beast as he left her, and Beauty's dreams that night were full of this strange, sad monster who seemed so hateful and yet so full of hurt; so eager to please and so easy to pain.

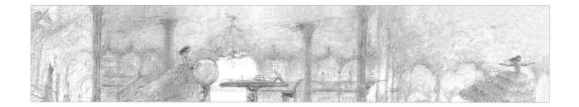

The next day and the days after it were as full of wonder and surprise for Beauty as her first. Her rooms never ceased to delight and amaze her, and there always seemed to be another one to discover.

There were rooms for the day and rooms for the night, rooms for every whim or pleasure.

There was the sewing room, in which she practiced embroidery and made fine tapestries. All the needles there threaded themselves for her convenience, and no pin ever pricked her thumb.

There was the aviary, filled with birds that sang the mysterious songs of the sky as they built their elaborate nests, and where she made friends with a splendid parrot who perched on her shoulder.

There was the monkey room, where she laughed until she wept at the antics of the chimpanzees, and the hammock room, and the painting room, and the extraordinary window room that every day had a different view of the gardens, no matter how often she visited it.

Then there were the gardens themselves, which looked even more astonishing now that the snow had all melted away and their full glory could be seen blossoming in the warm sunshine.

Beauty would ride or walk for hours, or, on lazy afternoons, lie back in a boat while the winding river carried her along, past meadows and orchards, pagodas, pavilions, and knot gardens.

There were fountains to splash in and waterfalls to sit beneath, mazes to explore, trees to climb, and the stunning colors of a million flowers to dazzle the eye.

Everywhere, proud, strutting peacocks spread their magnificent tails, chattering excitedly among themselves at Beauty's approach, and shy young deer learned to nuzzle her curiously with their warm, wet noses as the days passed into weeks, and the weeks into months, and they lost their fear of the stranger in their midst.

Nor was Beauty afraid anymore: she knew the Beast would not hurt her. He was never anything but courteous and kind, and concerned only for her happiness. She had even grown used to his looks—his thick mane of hair; his long, clawed fingers; the strangely shy way he walked. They never met by day, but each evening, as the clock struck nine, he would appear and ask if he might join her at her meal. Far from dreading his visits, Beauty found herself looking forward to them with pleasure, for he was good company. She had grown to like him more than she had ever imagined possible.

There was only one problem. Every evening, without fail, the Beast would ask her the same terrible question: "Will you marry me?" It was the one thing Beauty dreaded above all. She knew she must say no, and she knew how much it hurt him as he turned away, always with that heart-rending sigh. But still he would ask again the next night, and the night after, like a starving man torturing himself with dreams of food.

After three months, Beauty could bear it no longer. "Beast," she said

that evening, "please don't ask me again. It upsets me so much to cause you pain, but I can never love you. I treasure you as a dear, kind friend. Please be happy with that, and do not spoil it by wanting more."

The Beast was silent for a time, his head bowed. "I would not hurt you for any price," he said at last. "Forgive me." He raised his eyes to Beauty, and for a moment she feared that she had wounded him beyond repair, so broken and hopeless did he seem. But then he seemed to find courage, and somehow she knew what he would say even before he spoke. "I will not ask you again—I promise. Your company is a greater blessing than I ever hoped for. I ask only one thing: if you are happy to be my friend, please promise that you will never leave me alone."

Beauty was deeply touched and would willingly have granted his request, but she could not. That very morning she had seen in the magic mirror that her father was desperately ill with worry about her, and she longed to go home and nurse him. "I cannot be happy here," she explained, "while my father is sick. My heart aches for him."

"And my heart aches for you," said the Beast at once. "But if I send you to your father, you will surely stay there, and then your poor Beast will die of grief."

He looked so sad sitting there. She reached forward and touched his paw where it lay heavy on the table. "Dear Beast," she said. It was the first time she had ever felt the rough, coarse fur, and she was amazed to see how pale and delicate her hand looked against it. "I will not stay there," she said softly. "I promise to come back. I only want to make sure that my father is all right and to show him that I am well and happy. One week—then I will return."

Gently she stroked his paw, then carefully removed her hand, for the Beast was trembling in a kind of torment and twisting his head from side to side. When at last he stilled himself, his words were so quiet that Beauty had to lean forward to hear.

"You will be there tomorrow when you wake," he said in a flat, exhausted tone. There was no hope or happiness in it. She knew only that he had made a decision beyond her understanding, and that it had cost him dearly. Then he reached out toward her. "Keep this ring safe," he said, handing her a simple gold band.

"Place it on your pillow when you wish to return. But I beg you not to forget your promise—one week."

And then, before she could say anything, the Beast walked away, with a sigh more sad and weary than any she had ever heard him utter, pausing only for one long, last look at Beauty before he disappeared.

Beauty cried herself to sleep that night, for it was awful to be so fond of the Beast and to cause him such pain, but when she woke the next morning all thoughts of sadness disappeared at once. She was, to her sheer delight and wonder, in her old bed at home, with the sun shining in the window, and outside the fields stretching into the distance, rich with crops ready for harvest.

Beauty ran downstairs to the parlor and there was Mr. Fortune, scarcely able to believe his eyes at the sight of his beloved daughter. They hugged, laughing and weeping, and the tears seemed to wash the lines of worry and age from old Mr. Fortune's face until his cheeks glistened with a happiness that Beauty could scarcely remember.

Eventually, Hermione and Gertrude appeared as well. They had been woken by the noise of Beauty and her father dancing for joy, and both of them were in extremely bad tempers. "Be quiet, can't you," snapped Hermione. "Some of us are trying to sleep," added Gertrude, before they both stared at Beauty and said, disgustedly, "What are you doing here?"

Their moods were not improved when Beauty told them. In fact, they were furious. It was just so unfair. Here they were, stuck in the country, living the most tedious life imaginable with a dull, old father who spent all his time sick with worry, while their horrid little sister, who deserved to die for her stupidity, was luxuriating in a magical palace, waited on hand and foot, with no end of riches and entertainments to amuse her. Oh, they hated her, the ghastly little minx, but soon they worked out a way to get back at her.

"Let's make her stay," said Hermione, "for more than a week."

Gertrude clapped her hands with pleasure. "Oh, yes," she said, smiling. "That will make the Beast so angry that—"

"That it might kill her," Hermione spat viciously.

"But what can we do? How can we do it?" asked Gertrude.

"Let's pretend that we're pleased to see her," said Hermione. "She won't be able to resist."

From that moment on, Beauty's sisters treated her with such a show of love and kindness that she was quite overwhelmed. They brought her tea in bed; they laughed at all her jokes (and then they scowled behind her back).

Mr. Fortune was quite recovered as well, and Beauty was so happy that she knew it would be hard to leave, though she did miss the Beast a great deal.

On the morning she was meant to go, however, Hermione and Gertrude burst into tears and wept uncontrollably, pleading with Beauty to stay and think of them and their poor, dear father. Little did Beauty know that they had rubbed their eyes with onions to make themselves cry, but it was so convincing that Beauty, moved by their tears, agreed to stay a day longer.

Each morning, Beauty's sisters rubbed their eyes with onions until the false tears came, and each night they wept with laughter at the success of their plan, and every day Beauty agreed to stay a little longer, though she worried more and more about her promise to the Beast and was troubled by a strange sadness whenever she thought of him.

It was on her tenth night at home that Beauty finally understood what she had done. In the mirror, as she brushed her hair before bed, her reflection disappeared and she saw instead, as if from a great height, the Beast's palace bathed in pale moonlight, and then suddenly there was the Beast himself, lying beside the river in a part of the garden Beauty had never seen. He looked ill and wretched, and his eyes were full of a hopeless agony that Beauty knew was all her fault.

For a moment, she was unable to breathe with the shock. *I must go at once,* she thought. *I have hurt him; I have stayed away too long. Forgive me, Beast. I am coming.*

Quickly she laid the ring he had given her on her pillow, and the next thing she knew, it was morning, and she was waking up in the splendor of her bed in the Beast's palace. But it was colder than she remembered, and as she looked out of the window, she saw that snow had fallen and the trees were bare against a gray sky. Her rooms seemed cheerless and faded, like a song that has lost its tune.

Beauty could not settle, for she longed to see the Beast again and she was so excited at the prospect that the day passed all too slowly. As evening fell, she put on the most beautiful dress she could find, hoping nervously that it would please him, but there was no food laid out on the table when she went down, and when at last the longed-for hour approached and the clock struck nine, the Beast did not appear.

Now panic seized Beauty's heart like a cold fist. What was wrong? Where was he? He would die of grief, he had said, if she did not return, but surely those were just words. She was here now. She needed him. "Beast!" she shouted, running through the palace as fast as she could. "Beast, I'm here!" But every room was locked and silent, and only her echoes answered, with their false, fading life.

Frantically, Beauty tried to think. She must find him before it was too late. Outside—he'd been outside in the mirror. But everything was strange in the dark night as she ran, stumbling and calling, tears pouring down her cheeks, until at last she could run no more and she fell, her heart thumping against her chest, and howled her grief at the cruel moon.

And then she saw him. He lay by the river just as he had the night before, silent and unmoving. Snow had begun to settle on him like a

blanket, softening his shape, burying him in its cold, gentle flakes. "No," sobbed Beauty, "no, Beast, no!" She hurled herself across his body, desperately brushing the snow away, knowing that she was losing him, feeling him slip away. "Don't go, Beast," she cried. "I'm here, stay with me, don't go." But she knew it was hopeless, even as the Beast stirred one last time, his eyes flickering open.

He looked at her, and Beauty would have given anything to keep him there. "You broke your promise," he said faintly. "It is too late. But you have come, and I die happy because I have seen you again."

Then his eyes closed, and Beauty stared in horror as his body went limp in her arms. "No!" she cried, hot tears running down her cheeks and onto his face. "Not now. Please not now. Listen to me, Beast. You must not die. I love you. Stay with me. Beast, I love you."

Beauty was sobbing uncontrollably now. She had found love and lost it, and it was so much more than she had ever imagined, and the pain was unbearable. He was ugly, but he was beautiful—the most beautiful thing she had ever known—and now she couldn't tell him how she loved his eyes and his mouth and his crooked nose, his shy kindness and the way he walked and his huge hands, because he had slipped away. "I love you," she cried, and her eyes were swimming with tears and the white snow was dazzling and he had gone. "*I love you*," she repeated, as if words would bring him back when the world was melting with grief and her heart bursting with pain, and it was too late and she felt herself slipping down and dissolving into sorrow.

Only now someone was lifting her and snow was falling on her cheek, but it was warm like tears, and someone was whispering in her ear and gently asking,

"Then will you marry me?"
"Oh, yes, I will," she said, "oh, yes."

"Then open your eyes," she heard, and as Beauty blinked away her tears, it seemed to her that the sky was filled with dazzling light, and before her was no beast but a handsome prince whose dark eyes she knew and loved and in which she wanted to stay forever.

"Now you see me as I really am," he said. "Your love has saved me from a terrible spell. I was turned into a beast, and only a heart that loved me for my self could set me free."

"Well, you are very handsome now," said Beauty, with a smile, "but I loved you anyway, the way you were." She stroked his smooth cheeks and his strong hands, pleased to see that his nose was still a little bent and his eyes just as deep, for he looked so much more interesting than the picture-book prince she had always imagined. "And I love you now," she added, leaning forward to kiss him, "more than words can ever say."

And very soon afterward they were married, and of course they lived happily ever after, for they had earned their love, and love that is earned lasts a very long time, and about that there really is no more to say.

But there are some pictures of the wedding and of the happy couple walking arm in arm—the delighted Mr. Fortune will show them to you, beaming with pride, at any opportunity you give him. "Aren't they splendid?" he'll say, unable to contain himself. "Always knew she'd make an excellent match. Best son-in-law you could hope for. Happiest day of my life. Helped introduce them myself. Fabulous gardener. Brilliant with his roses. You know how they met, of course? No? Have I never told you the story of

Beauty and the Beast

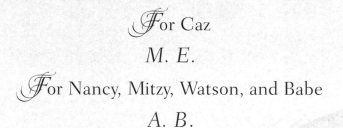

For Caz
M. E.
For Nancy, Mitzy, Watson, and Babe
A. B.

First U.S. edition 2006

Library of Congress Cataloging-in-Publication Data

Eilenberg, Max
Beauty and the beast / retold by Max Eilenberg ; illustrated by Angela Barrett. — 1st U.S. ed.
p.   cm.
Summary: Through her great capacity to love, a kind and beautiful maid
releases a handsome prince from the spell that has made him an ugly beast.
ISBN-10: 0-7636-3160-4
ISBN-13: 978-0-7636-3160-4
[1. Fairy tales. 2. Folklore—France.]
I. Barrett, Angela, ill. II. Beauty and the beast. English. III. Title.
PZ8.E355Be 2007
398.20944'01—dc22   2006043171

2 4 6 8 10 9 7 5 3 1

Printed in China

This book was typeset in Fairfield Light.
The illustrations were done in watercolor.

Candlewick Press
2067 Massachusetts Avenue
Cambridge, Massachusetts 02140

visit us at www.candlewick.com

For Mom

All rights reserved. Published in the United States by Random House Children's Books,
a division of Penguin Random House LLC, New York.
Random House and the colophon are registered trademarks of Penguin Random House LLC.
Visit us on the Web! randomhousekids.com
Educators and librarians, for a variety of teaching tools, visit us at RHTeachersLibrarians.com
Library of Congress Cataloging-in-Publication Data
Names: Bramsen, Carin, author.
Title: Sleepover Duck! / by Carin Bramsen.
Description: First edition. | New York : Random House Children's Books |2018|
Summary: Duck and Cat have their very first sleepover in the barn.
Identifiers: LCCN 2016046616 (print) | LCCN 2017021107 (ebook)
ISBN 978-0-385-38417-9 (hc) | ISBN 978-0-375-97345-1 (glb) | ISBN 978-0-385-38418-6 (ebook)
Subjects: | CYAC: Stories in rhyme. | Sleepovers—Fiction. | Ducks—Fiction. | Cats—Fiction. |
Friendship—Fiction. | Domestic animals—Fiction.
Classification: LCC PZ8.3.B7324 (ebook) | LCC PZ8.3.B7324 S| 2017 (print) | DDC [E]—dc23
MANUFACTURED IN CHINA
10 9 8 7 6 5 4 3 2 1   First Edition
Book design by Tracy Tyler